THE CHILDREN'S CLASSICS
Collection

Dados Internacionais de Catalogação na Publicação (CIP) de acordo com ISBD

N458t Nesbit, Edith

The Railway Children / Edith Nesbit. - Jandira, SP : W. Books, 2025.
120 p. : 12,80cm x 19,80cm. - (Classics).

ISBN: 978-65-5294-119-0

1. Literatura inglesa. 2. Aventura. 3. História. 4. Emoções. 5. Clássicos. I. Título. II. Série.

2025-2481 CDD 823.91
CDU 821.111-3

Elaborada por Lucio Feitosa - CRB-8/8803
Índice para catálogo sistemático:
1. Literatura inglesa 823.91
2. Literatura inglesa 821.111-3

Text based on the original story by Edith Nesbit,
adapted by Gemma Barder
Illustrations by Archina Laezza

1st edition in 2025
www.cirandacultural.com.br

The Railway Children

Edith Nesbit

W. Books

Roberta (Bobbie)
The eldest sister

Peter
The middle child

Phyllis
The youngest sister

Mother

Father

Perks
The station porter

Doctor Forrest
A doctor

The Old Gentleman
A kindly man who waves from the train

Chapter One

They were not always the Railway Children. In fact, the railway meant nothing to them at first, except as a way of getting to the theatre or the seaside.

Roberta was twelve and the eldest of the three children. Everyone called her Bobbie, so that's what we shall do. She was kind, responsible and thoughtful. Next

came Peter, who was nearly ten. He liked solving problems and finding out how things worked. Lastly, there was Phyllis, who was eight and always meant well – even if she did not always get things right first time.

They lived in London, in a smart red-brick house with their mother and father, a cook and two maids. They had everything they could ever wish for. Mother was not one of those boring mothers who spent all day paying calls on other women; she was fun and loved to play with her children when she was not teaching them their lessons. She made up excellent stories too. Their father was just perfect. He was tall and clever, never too cross or too easy going, and he always had time for a game or to answer any questions they threw at him.

Life for Bobbie, Peter and Phyllis was just wonderful, but they did not realise quite *how* wonderful it was until the day everything became just dreadful.

It happened on Peter's tenth birthday. He had been given something he'd always wanted – a miniature train engine that chugged around the living room, puffing out real steam. The whole family enjoyed watching the train,

until suddenly it stopped. The engine clanked and rattled and let out the most awful smell. 'Oh, Father,' cried Peter, cradling the engine with a tear in his eye. 'Is there any hope for it?'

'Hope?' replied Father, cheerfully. 'There's always hope! I shall put Saturday afternoon aside for it and you shall all help me fix it.'

'Even the girls?' said Peter.

'Especially the girls,' said Father.

‘Remember, each of you can do anything you put your mind to!’

Peter was just starting to feel better about his broken engine, when there was a knock at the front door. The family looked at each other in surprise, not knowing who could be calling.

It was after dinner, and Mother was just about to usher the children to bed. Ruth, one of the family's maids, answered the door. They heard male voices talking in the hallway. A moment or two later, Ruth came into the living room looking pale and serious. 'There are two men to see you, sir,' she told Father. 'I've shown them into the library.'

Chapter Two

The children stayed up to say goodnight to Father. They waited impatiently while he was talking to the men in the library. Mother went to see what was happening. After what seemed like a lifetime, the children heard footsteps in the hallway and the front door opened and closed.

'Finally!' said Phyllis. 'Now Daddy can read us a bedtime story!'

Mother came back into the living room. Her face was as white as the lace on her dress. 'My dears,' she said, quietly. 'I'm afraid Daddy has had to go away … on business.'

Bobbie stared at her mother in concern. Her eyes were rimmed with red, and it looked as though she had been crying.

'Now, up to bed with you all. I shall be up in a moment to tuck you in,' she said. Bobbie waited as Phyllis and Peter trotted up the stairs and were out of earshot.

earshot

The distance over which sound, like a voice or a noise, can be heard by a person.

'No one has died, have they Mummy?' she asked.

Mother smiled, sadly. 'No, my darling, no one has died,' she replied. 'But I can't tell you anything about it tonight. Be a good girl and go up to bed.'

After that night, things continued to get worse. Mother was out from first thing in the morning until late at night every single day.

She would come home exhausted and only had time to kiss each child on the head before bed.

Weeks passed, and Father still did not come home. The maids and cook were sent away, and their Aunt Emma came to help. Aunt Emma was stern and certainly not as loving as their mother.

She was due to go to India to be a governess for a very important family, but she was a great help to Mother – and for that the children were very grateful.

governess

A woman employed to educate and train the children of a private household.

One morning, after Mother had been away for a whole week, she gathered Bobbie, Peter and Phyllis in the living room. She looked tired and pale, but her face lit up with a smile when she saw the children. She sat next to them on the sofa and wrapped her arms around all three of them. 'Now then, my

dears,' she began, brightly. 'We are off on an adventure! We are going to live in the countryside in Yorkshire, in a sweet little cottage called the Three Chimneys. I'll need you to pack only the things you really need, as the cottage is much smaller than our house here.'

Although the children were frightened and quite upset to be leaving the only home they had ever known, they knew they had to be brave for Mother.

'Do you know where Father is, Bobbie?' Phyllis asked, as she packed her favourite dolls into a box.

'No,' replied Bobbie, sadly. 'And we must not ask Mother. It will only make her sad.'

'But what if he's trapped somewhere? Or lost?' Phyllis said.

'Then he will find his way back to us,' said Bobbie. 'I am certain of it.'

Chapter Three

With the help of Aunt Emma and her clipboard, the red-brick house was packed up. Bobbie looked at the small amount of furniture and boxes that they were taking with them. She could not believe that their whole lives could be made into something so little.

'Do you each have a handkerchief?' asked Aunt Emma, as she helped them find their platform at King's Cross station.

She was boarding her boat to India the next day, and this was the last time they would see her.

'Yes, Aunt Emma,' the children said together. Aunt Emma always insisted on them having a clean white handkerchief at all times. In a way, they were sad to see her leave. Apart from Mother, Aunt Emma was the last reminder of their old life in London. Now, as they waited to board their train, none of them knew when or if they might come home again, or when they might see Father.

The train journey to Yorkshire

took a long time. Each of the children soon fell into a bumpy sleep. When they woke, it was dark outside, and the windows had turned into mirrors.

‘Here we are, my darlings!’ said Mother cheerfully, as the train came to a halt. ‘We have arrived!’

The family stepped dozily onto the cold platform, which was lit by a single lamp. A horse and cart stood at one end, with their furniture and belongings piled up high on the back thanks to the friendly porter. There were no cabs from the tiny station at that time of night, so Mother, Bobbie, Peter and Phyllis clutched their suitcases and trudged behind the cart. It was so

porter

A person employed to carry luggage, parcels or supplies, especially at a railway station or hotel.

dark that they could hardly see one foot in front of the other, which was strange for three children so used to the streetlights in London.

More than once, Phyllis stumbled and screamed, and the family had to stop while she got herself together.

Just when they thought they would never reach the house, a cloud moved away from the moon

and revealed a white cottage on a hill. Their spirits lifted for a moment, as the house really did look like something from a storybook. It was small but welcoming, and they could not wait to get inside, have some food and go to bed.

'Where is Mrs Viney?' asked Mother, as she walked along the small path to the front door. 'She was meant to get the house ready for us, but it's all dark and locked up.'

'Key'll be under the mat,' said the cart driver. 'Thas 'ow we do it up our way.'

Sure enough, Mother found the key and opened the door, which led into a small kitchen. A single candle on the side provided just enough light for their furniture to

be brought in by the cart driver and Mother. The children carried in the smaller items, so the job didn't take too long.

'It's cold,' moaned Peter.

'And what's that scurrying sound?' asked Bobbie.

The driver laughed as he dumped the final box at their feet. 'Only the rats!' he said, before leaving the family alone.

'Mrs Viney was meant to set out our supper, but there's nothing here!' said Mother, sounding as close to angry as she ever got.

They explored the downstairs rooms of the house, which did not take long. As well as the kitchen, there was a dining room and a living room. Each room was filled with the few pieces of furniture the family had brought with them, but Bobbie thought everything looked strange against the walls of the new house.

'Find the box of kitchen things!' Mother said at last. 'Aunt Emma packed all the old tins and bits and pieces from the cupboards. We'll find some supper in there, I'm sure.'

So, on their first night at the

Three Chimneys, the family sat down to a feast of biscuits, sardines, raisins, ginger, marmalade and lime cordial. They ate off saucers and drank out of teacups, as no plates or glasses could be found in the dark.

As Bobbie sipped lime cordial from her teacup, she realised just how different their lives would be from now on.

Chapter Four

In the morning, Bobbie woke Phyllis and Peter extra early. She was sharing a room with Phyllis now, so it was easy to tiptoe over to her bed and gently shake her awake. Then the two of them crept along the upstairs corridor to Peter's small box room.

'We should help unpack before Mother gets up,' Bobbie whispered, and Peter instantly agreed.

In the daylight, the cottage looked much better than the night before. There were no rats, and the house stood on a hill overlooking the countryside and the railway line just beyond. 'Let's go and explore!' said Peter.

‘Okay,’ Bobbie agreed. ‘But just for a little while, and not too far.’ She still wanted to surprise Mother by unpacking the boxes before she woke up.

An hour later, the boxes had still not been unpacked. Mother found her three children in the back garden, fast asleep in the sunshine. She woke them up with a smile and told them they were having chicken pie and apple crumble for breakfast.

‘Pie?’ squealed Phyllis. ‘For breakfast?’

'You know that door in the kitchen we all thought was a cupboard?' began Mother. 'It turns out it is a breakfast room. Mrs Viney *had* set out everything we needed for our supper after all. She left a note on the door to say that she had to go home early because her daughter was sick. It was so dark that we didn't find the note or the room!'

After breakfast, the family set about making the house their own. Phyllis felt as though she were setting up a giant doll's house, while

Peter tried his best to light a fire in each room.

Later, Mrs Viney came round to cook dinner and re-do the fires properly so that the house was as cosy as could be. That night, the children slept heavily.

The next morning, Mother asked the children to play outside while she worked. She had decided to try and sell some of her stories to a children's magazine, and needed quiet while she wrote them.

The children decided to explore the steep hill that ran down to the railway line. 'It's far bigger than the track that went around our old living room,' said Phyllis, thinking back to the night Father had left them.

In the distance, they could see a train winding its way through the countryside. 'That train's going to London,' said Peter, decisively.

'Daddy's in London!' cried Phyllis, excitedly.

'We don't know that, Phyl,' said Bobbie. 'But he could be.'

'I think we should ask the train to send our love to Father,' said Phyllis.

Bobbie looked at Phyllis for a moment. 'Yes, why not,' she said.

As the train rumbled past, the children waved their handkerchiefs from Aunt Emma in the air and shouted, 'Send our love to Father!' At the end of the train, they spotted an old gentleman. He smiled at them and happily waved his newspaper back.

Chapter Five

The children only knew of two places in the village: the Three Chimneys and the station. So, they decided to walk to the station to see if it looked different in the daylight. It did. It was much more

welcoming, with hanging baskets of pink and purple flowers and a white wooden trim. A smart-looking man in uniform paced up and down the platform. It was the porter who had helped them with their furniture.

‘How do you do?’ said Peter, introducing himself in a way he had seen Father do many times. ‘We’ve just moved into the Three Chimneys. I don’t suppose you can fix engines?’

The porter looked from Peter to Bobbie to Phyllis. ‘I might,’ he said. ‘But I’m far better with a train timetable.’

‘Then you are a good person to know,’ said Bobbie. ‘I’m Roberta, but everyone calls me Bobbie, and this is Phyllis and Peter.’

‘Nice to meet you. I’m Perks,’ said the porter, tipping the front of his little blue cap towards the children. 'Now, if you don't mind, the 10.55 is due any minute, but if you bring me that engine, I might be able to take a look at it.' With that, Perks trotted to the end of the platform to wave his little flag and blow his whistle. '10.55 from York to Whitby!' he shouted. The children knew instantly that they were going to like Perks.

As the days passed by, the family settled into the gentle rhythm of their new life. The children had many more chores than before, but they liked to keep busy. Mrs Viney was at the house most days, and when Mother was not writing, she was teaching them as she always did. Occasionally they would mention Father, but they talked as though he had just gone to work or popped to the shops. None of the children asked Mother where he was, or when he would be coming back in case it upset her.

Every morning, the children would run down to the track to see the 9.15 train to London. They always waved and sent their love to Father. More and more passengers began to wave back – including the Old Gentleman, who always sat in the last carriage and waved with his newspaper.

One morning, the children had just returned home, expecting to start their lessons, to find Mother still in bed. She was sitting up, a shawl around her shoulders and a cup of hot lemon in her hands. Her hair was not pinned up in its usual elegant way, and her nose was bright red. 'No lessons today, I'm afraid,' Mother said, stopping to cough so violently that Phyllis hid behind Peter. 'Bobbie, run

and fetch Doctor Forrest from the village. I'm sure he will have something to get me up and about in no time.'

Bobbie ran through the village to the house with a small brass plaque on the door that read: *DR FORREST*. The kindly doctor drove Bobbie back to the Three Chimneys in his own pony and cart, and saw to Mother straight away.

The children sat in the living room, each deciding what they could do to help Mother get better. After about twenty minutes, the doctor came in with a list of food, drink and medicine. 'Roberta,

I am making you head nurse,' he said, handing her the list with a smile. 'It's just a spot of flu. If she rests and takes everything on this list, she'll be herself in a week or so.'

'Thank you, Doctor Forrest,' said Bobbie, suddenly feeling very grown up.

Chapter Six

'We can't buy all this!' said Mother, handing the list back to Bobbie the following morning. 'All I need is some sweet tea and a day in bed and I'll be fine.'

'But the doctor said you need medicine,' Bobbie said, worriedly.

Mother placed a hand on her arm. 'Darling, we just can't afford it right now. Not until I've sold some more stories.'

Bobbie trudged downstairs and

into the garden, where Peter and Phyllis were making a hedgehog house out of sticks. 'I told you she'd say no,' said Peter.

'We just *have* to get all the things on the list,' said Bobbie. 'Everybody, think and don't speak until we come up with an idea.'

Nobody spoke for a full five minutes, until Phyllis suddenly jumped up and cried, 'Perks!'

'Don't be silly,' said Peter. 'Perks can't buy Mother's medicine. I think he might be poorer than we are.'

Bobbie frowned at Peter for

being rude about their new friend.

Phyllis shook her head. 'Perks was telling me about the Old Gentleman we wave to. He's rich. He's in charge of the railway, or part of it at least.'

Bobbie stood up. 'Oh, Phyl,' she said. 'What a brilliant idea. But we mustn't tell Mother. She won't like us asking a stranger for things.'

Bobbie, Peter and Phyllis ran to the garden shed, where they knew there was an old sheet and tins of leftover paint. Taking great care to avoid getting paint on their clothes, they made a sign.

While the paint was still wet, they ran to the hill to wait for the 9.15 train to London. As usual, the Old Gentleman waved at them with his newspaper. He stopped when he saw that Peter and Phyllis were pointing at their sign, which read: *LOOK OUT AT THE STATION!*

When the train pulled into the station, the Old Gentleman popped

his head out of his carriage window and saw Bobbie waiting for him. She handed him a note before the train pulled off again. It read:

Dear Mr we do not know your name,

Mother is ill and the doctor says to give her the things at the end of this letter, but she says she can't afford it. We do not know anybody here but you, because Father is away and we do not know where. Father will pay you, or if he has lost all his money we will pay you back when we are grown up and have jobs of our own.

From, Roberta, Phyllis and Peter
(the children who wave).

They had no clue if their idea would work. The Old Gentleman might think them rude for asking, but they would never know unless they tried. The following day, just as they were packing up their breakfast things, Perks knocked at the door. 'Got a delivery for you,' he said, cheerfully. He handed a large wicker basket to Bobbie. 'Your Old Gentleman said to give this to the children up at Three Chimneys.'

Bobbie's faced flushed with delight when she saw the basket. It was full of medicine, packets

of tea and powders for hot drinks, as well as a bunch of flowers. And along with it there was a note:

> Dear Roberta, Phyllis and Peter,
>
> Here are the things you need. Your mother will want to know where they came from. Tell her they were sent by a friend who heard she was ill. When she is well again, you must tell her all about it, of course. And if she says you ought not to have asked for the things, tell her that I say you were quite right, and that I hope she will forgive me for taking the liberty of allowing myself a very great pleasure.
>
> G. P.

Chapter Seven

Mother was well again within a week. The children knew they had to do what the Old Gentleman

had asked and tell her the truth about where the food and medicine had come from. At first, Mother was cross with the children for asking a stranger for help, but she softened a little when she read the Old Gentleman's letter.

Mother was now so well that she began to take weekly trips to London. She told the children that she was 'running errands', but they secretly thought her trips had something to do with Father – though they never asked. Each of the children missed him terribly. Sometimes they would talk about the fun they used to have together, and it would make them cry, but they made sure to dry their eyes before going in to see Mother again.

It was late evening when the three children were waiting for

Mother's train from London to come into the station. 'We got here too early,' said Peter, studying the timetable on the waiting room noticeboard. 'There's one more train to come before Mother's.'

As the children waited for the passengers to file through the station, they heard concerned voices. A man had collapsed on the platform. He had a beard and long hair that hung in strings around his shoulders. His clothes were covered in patches, and he looked tired and hungry. Nobody could understand a word he said.

'E's speaking German!' someone said.

'That's not German,' said Peter, pushing his way to the front of the crowd.

'What is it then, smarty-pants?'

Peter frowned. 'I don't know. I can only speak a bit of French, and that isn't French.'

The man's eyes lit up. 'Francais?' he said.

'*That's* French!' said Peter, triumphantly.

With Perks's help, the children took the man to the waiting room.

When Mother's train pulled into the station, Bobbie rushed to fetch her, speaking as fast as she could. 'There's a man, we don't know where he's from, but he can speak French, and you can speak French, and he's in the waiting room!'

As soon as Mother began to speak French to the man, he grabbed Mother's arm. A short while later, he was crying and smiling all at the same time.

'How odd,' said Phyllis. 'I can't work out if he is happy or sad.'

‘Happy, I think,’ said Bobbie.

The man came back to the Three Chimneys with Mother and the children. He was given Peter’s box room to sleep in, which Peter felt very proud of – even if it meant sleeping on the sofa in Bobbie and Phyllis’s room.

After the man had gone to bed, Mother gathered the children in their bedroom. ‘My dears, the gentleman is a famous Russian writer!’ she said. ‘He wrote a book that the Russian government did not like, so he and his family had to run away. But he got separated from his wife and children on the journey. He’s been searching for them ever since. I think we must help him, if you agree?’

The children nodded their heads in unison.

Chapter Eight

The Russian's name was Szezcpansky, though Phyllis always pronounced it 'She-pants-eve'. He was a very nice man, even though he could only speak to Mother in French.

He told her all about his life and his family. Doctor Forrest came to look him over, and thankfully he did not need a basketful of medicine. He just needed some rest and good food, which the family were happy to provide despite not having much themselves.

One evening, after Szezcpansky had gone to bed, Bobbie crept into Mother's room with tears in her eyes. 'Mother, Daddy isn't … dead, is he?' she asked.

'My darling, no! Of course he isn't!' Mother said, wrapping Bobbie up in her arms. 'Why would you think such a thing?'

Bobbie let her tears fall. 'Because Mr Szezcpansky is wearing Daddy's clothes,' she said, miserably. 'If

Daddy was alive somewhere, surely he would need his clothes?'

Mother sighed. 'I am sorry that I haven't told you where Daddy is,' she said. 'But will you trust me when I tell you that the last time I saw Daddy, he was well and misses you all dreadfully. Please don't ask me to tell you any more.'

Bobbie nodded her head and gave Mother a big hug. It was enough to know for now.

One thing Szezcpansky loved more than anything was fresh strawberries. The children remembered that Perks had told them about a patch of wild strawberries that grew just along the hill from their own house, so they grabbed a basket from the kitchen and went to investigate.

After a short walk, followed by a prickly search through the bushes, the children were ready to go home – but with no strawberries in their basket.

'Look at that!' said Phyllis. She was staring wide-eyed at the hill on the other side of the railway tracks. 'It's like magic!'

Bobbie and Peter followed Phyllis's gaze, and for a moment they were stunned into silence. The trees on the hill seemed to be moving, all by themselves, down the hill towards the track. Huge rocks and mud soon followed, until a big pile of debris completely covered the tracks.

'It's a landslide!' said Bobbie.

'What are we going to do?' cried Peter. 'The express train will be along in ten minutes! It's going to plough straight into it!'

The children dropped their basket and began to run. 'Let's go to the station and warn Perks,' said Bobbie.

'It'll be too late by then!' said Peter.

'Why don't we wave to get them to stop?' suggested Phyllis.

'No one will take any notice – we always wave!' said Peter. 'We've got to do something! We need something red. Red means danger.'

'We can use our petticoats!' cried Phyllis, shimmying out of her red, flannel petticoat. Bobbie copied her little sister as they raced

down the hill. Peter scrambled about, searching for sticks. Soon, they heard the train's familiar whistle as it came around the bend.

Chapter Nine

'It's not going to stop!' cried Bobbie, waving her red petticoat on the end of one of the sticks Peter had found. 'We're too far away!'

Phyllis waved her flag and Peter jumped up and down, desperately. 'What can we do?' said Phyllis, tears filling her eyes.

'We have to get closer!' said Bobbie, running onto the track.

'No, Bobbie!' yelled Peter,

terrified that his sister might get run over by the speeding train.

But Bobbie's plan was working. The train driver had seen her, and the train's brakes were screeching horribly. The train had been going so fast that it was taking a long time to slow down.

It was getting closer and closer to Bobbie, but she refused to move off the track. The train finally came to a stop, just metres from where Bobbie stood. Overwhelmed by both fear and relief, Bobbie collapsed onto the track.

After a moment of frightened silence, the air was filled with commotion. Phyllis began to cry, and the train driver and conductor were shouting at all three children. 'What are you playing at!?' yelled the driver.

'You could have got yourselves killed!' shouted the conductor.

Peter ran as fast as he could to Bobbie. She slowly opened her eyes. 'Did we stop the train?' she asked.

Just then, the driver spotted the landslide on the tracks ahead. 'Blimey,' he said, taking off his hat and staring at the children. 'You've saved our lives.'

A few weeks later, Mother was standing in her best dress and hat, proudly watching Bobbie, Peter and Phyllis receive gold watches from the railway company for their bravery. A little stand had been set up at the station, with a brass band and a table of tea and cakes. The whole village had come out to watch. What made the day extra special was the fact that the Old

Gentleman, *their* Old Gentleman, had come to present the watches himself.

'I think this is the nicest present I have ever been given,' said Phyllis. 'Look! There's writing on the back.'

Inscribed on the back of each watch was:

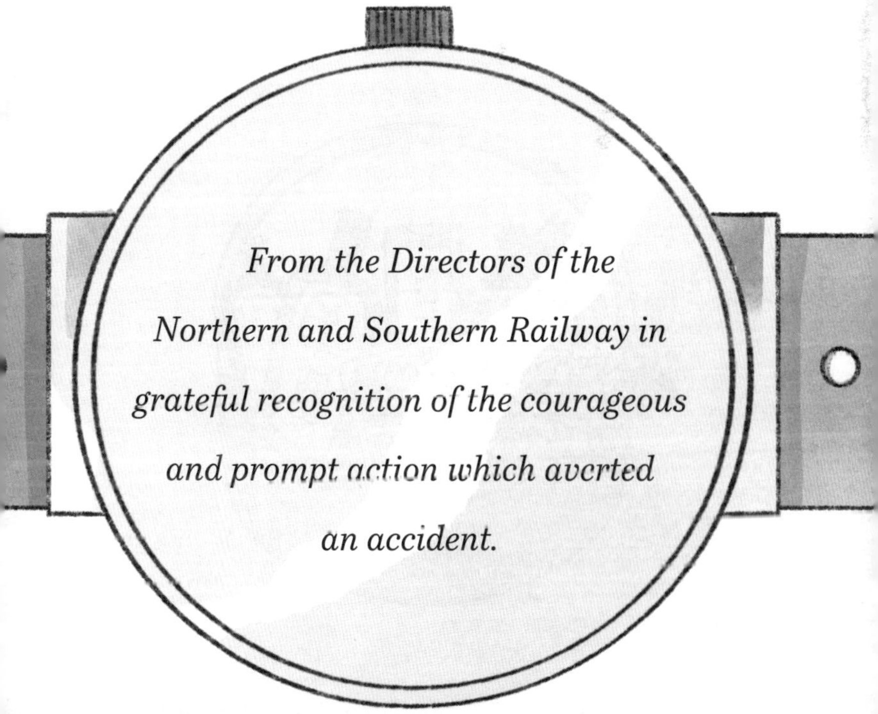

Mother was grateful that she finally had the chance to thank the Old Gentleman in person for the basket he had kindly sent her when she was poorly. As they were politely saying goodbye, Bobbie pressed another letter into his hand. He tipped his hat and promised to read it on the train ride home.

Chapter Ten

A week later, Bobbie was alone in the garden at the Three Chimneys. As she got older, she found that she sometimes liked to be away from her brother and sister. Although she loved them very much, she knew that she could think about Father when she was on her own, and cry if she needed to without any questions. Peter and Phyllis had stopped talking about Father as much as they used to, and she often worried that they might be forgetting him.

It was while she was deep in thought that a rather out of

breath Perks appeared at the garden gate.

'Perks!' Bobbie said, delighted. 'What are you doing here?'

'Just … had … word …' Perks began between breaths. 'The boss … is on his … way. Wants … to see … you.'

'The boss?' Bobbie furrowed her brow. 'You mean our Old Gentleman? How lovely!'

Bobbie skipped after Perks, back down into the village and into the station. They arrived just in time to see the Old Gentleman stepping off his train. He smiled broadly when he saw Bobbie. 'I have good news for you, young lady,' he said.

‘After I read your letter telling me all about your Russian visitor, I made some enquiries. I am pleased to say that we have found his family!’

Bobbie jumped up and down in excitement. ‘Oh! He will be so pleased!’

‘I could not resist coming to tell him the news in person,’ said the Old Gentleman.

Bobbie’s face fell. She was a little disappointed that she was not going to be the one to tell

enquiry

A question or request for more information.

Szezcpansky the good news, but of course it was the Old Gentleman who had done all the hard work.

'On second thoughts,' said the Old Gentleman, seeing Bobbie's face, 'perhaps it would be better coming from you? I am a stranger after all, and you must know him very well by now?'

Bobbie grinned and hugged the Old Gentleman. They took a cab back to the Three Chimneys. As soon as they arrived, Bobbie rushed to the garden where Szezcpansky and Mother were drinking tea. The Old Gentleman stood back at the garden gate and watched as Szezcpansky's eyes filled with happy tears. He hugged Bobbie, then Mother, then rushed to shake the Old Gentleman's hand.

Mother packed a trunk with some of Father's clothes, a couple of books and a few mementos of Szezcpansky's time at the Three Chimneys. Szezcpansky loaded the trunk onto the back of a cab. After hugging everyone one last time, he left the house to be reunited with his family.

Chapter Eleven

Although Peter was glad to have his room back, life seemed quiet at the Three Chimneys without Szezcpansky. So, they were very excited to hear that the local boys' school were putting on a paper chase that weekend.

'What *is* a paper chase?' asked Phyllis, spooning marmalade onto her toast one morning.

'Phyl, what have I said about putting butter *and* marmalade onto your toast?' said Mother, a little more crossly than usual. 'You know it is either one or the other. We cannot afford both.'

Phyllis sadly put down the marmalade spoon.

'I'm sorry, Phyl,' said Mother, smiling once again. 'I have sold three stories this week, so on Friday I'll go to the baker's and get buns for tea, I promise.'

Phyllis cheered up a bit after that, and Peter explained what a paper chase was.

'There's one boy in a white jersey,' he said, authoritatively. 'He's called the Hare. He starts first and runs around the countryside, leaving bits of paper behind him. Then there's a group of boys in red jerseys who must find him. They're called the Hounds.'

Phyllis frowned. 'That sounds like an awful lot of running to me,' she said.

'Of course it is! That's the point!' said Peter.

'Perks said they go past the hill,' said Bobbie. 'Let's go and watch after breakfast. I promise *you* won't have to run, Phyl.'

'I wish we were rich enough for butter *and* marmalade,' Phyllis sighed, flopping down on the hill and squinting into the sunshine.

'We used to be,' said Peter, with his hands on his hips. He was watching the horizon for any sign of the runners.

'I don't remember,' said Phyllis.

Bobbie sat next to her sister. 'Don't you?' she asked, concerned.

‘Phyl, you do remember Father, don’t you?’

Phyllis looked at her sister with wide eyes. ‘Of *course* I do! Why would you say such a thing?’

‘It’s just … you and Peter don’t talk about him anymore,’ said Bobbie. ‘None of us do.’

Phyllis and Peter exchanged a secretive look. ‘We decided to stop talking about him in case Mother got upset,’ Phyllis said.

Bobbie was just about to reply when Peter shouted, ‘Here they come!’

Bobbie and Phyllis jumped up

and watched as a boy in a white jersey ran along the hill. He had a small bag around his shoulder and was throwing handfuls of paper confetti behind him as he ran.

He stopped for a moment, deciding where to go next. Then he ran down the steep hill towards the railway line, and through the tunnel.

'What is he playing at?!' said Peter, sounding just like Perks. 'He can't lead a bunch of children down a railway tunnel!'

'There he goes!' said Phyllis, pointing to the boy in white as he ran off into the countryside.

Moments later, a group of boys in red appeared. Peter counted them before they followed the paper trail into the tunnel, and then he rushed to the other side.

'The 10.15 will be along in a minute!' said Bobbie, as she and Phyllis caught up to their brother. 'They need to hurry!'

As the boys ran out of the tunnel, Peter quickly counted them again. 'They haven't all come out,' he said. 'There's one still in there!'

Chapter Twelve

'Are you certain, Peter?' Bobbie asked.

'Of course I am!' Peter replied, offended. 'I *can* count you know.'

'Then we'll just have to go in and get him,' said Bobbie.

'You can't!' squealed Phyllis. 'It's too dangerous, and we promised Perks we would never go on the tracks again after the landslide.'

Bobbie shook her head. 'This is different. This is an emergency!'

A low moaning echoed through the tunnel. 'What was that?' gasped Phyllis. 'It sounded like a dragon!'

'How do you know what a dragon sounds like?' asked Peter. 'It was the boy, of course! He's obviously hurt himself and–' Peter stopped talking as he heard a low humming sound on the railway line.

The humming grew louder and louder, and then there came the

deafening whistle of the 10.15. 'Stand back!' Peter said. The children scrambled back up the hill, away from the tracks, and watched the train thunder through the tunnel.

'The boy's dead!' cried Phyllis. 'I just know he's dead!'

'Calm down, Phyl!' said Bobbie, trying to stop her voice from trembling. She took a deep breath. 'The next train's not for another hour. We have to go inside and see if he's all right.'

The children clung to each other as they entered the tunnel, staying as close to the sides as they could. Just as the outside light was growing dim, they saw the shape of a boy lying next to the track. 'There he is!' cried Bobbie, running ahead.

When they reached the boy, he looked up at them, obviously in pain. 'It's all right,' said Bobbie, soothingly. 'It's quite all right.'

'Is he dead?' said Phyllis, keeping her eyes shut tight. 'Is there a lot of blood?'

'Stop being such a goose,' said Peter. 'He's not dead, look!'

Phyllis slowly opened her eyes. The boy looked only a little older than Bobbie. 'It's my leg,' he gasped. 'I think it's broken.'

'You two run to the station; it's closer than home,' Bobbie told Peter and Phyllis. 'Find someone

to come and help. I'll stay with–'

she stopped, suddenly realising that she didn't know the boy's name. 'I'm so sorry that I haven't introduced myself. I'm Bobbie. This is my brother Peter, and that's our sister Phyl.'

Despite his pain, the boy smiled at the formal way Bobbie introduced herself. 'I'm Jim,' he replied. 'Your mother must have really liked boys' names.'

Phyllis giggled. 'I'm Phyllis, and that's Roberta, silly!' she said, before running back down the tunnel with Peter.

Bobbie knelt next to the boy and took her handkerchief out of her pocket. She began to dab gently at a graze on Jim's head. 'I'm awfully glad you came along,' he said.

Chapter Thirteen

Perks helped to settle Jim into bed while Doctor Forrest examined his leg. Mother brought bowls of clean water and a nightshirt for him to change into, and Peter was sent to Jim's school with a telegram to let them know what had happened.

Bobbie and Phyllis paced the living room, waiting to hear if Jim was going to be all right. Finally, Mother and Doctor Forrest entered. 'Well done, Head Nurse,' said Doctor Forrest, smiling at Bobbie. 'Thanks to you, Jim's leg is going to be all right. He just needs to rest for a while, and he'll soon be hobbling around on crutches. In the meantime, I've given your mother a new job – Matron of the Three Chimneys Hospital.'

Phyllis giggled at the doctor's joke, but Bobbie worried how Mother would manage to carry on writing and look after Jim. She decided she would help out as much as she could, which would not leave much time for playing with Peter and Phyllis. But it did mean that she would get to talk to Jim every day.

One morning, Bobbie went into the village to fetch a loaf of bread. She didn't normally pay much attention to the newspaper the bread was wrapped in, but today was different. Today, a picture of Father stared up at her.

Bobbie trembled as she unwrapped the loaf and smoothed out the paper. She read quickly, her

eyes darting over the article. She folded the paper and put it into the pocket of her dress.

Back at the Three Chimneys, Mother was in the kitchen. She was cheerful because she had just sold another story, and had decided that Phyllis could have marmalade *and* butter on her toast today. She looked up as Bobbie came into the room. 'Whatever is the matter, my darling?' asked Mother, taking in her daughter's pale face.

Wordlessly, Bobbie took the paper out of her pocket and handed it over. Mother's face turned white. She took Bobbie by the hand, and they sat together by the small kitchen fire.

'Is it true, Mother?' Bobbie said at last. 'Is Daddy in prison?'

Mother looked down. Tears filled her eyes but she refused to let them fall. 'Yes,' she replied, quietly.

'You don't believe he did the things they say he did, do you?' Bobbie cried.

'No!' Mother said, firmly. 'Of course not. Daddy is good and noble, and he belongs to us.' Mother hugged Bobbie tightly before explaining what had happened. 'Those men who came to the house accused Daddy of spying. Of giving away secrets to another country. They found evidence in his desk, but Daddy says it was put there to make him look guilty.'

'Who would do such a terrible thing?' Bobbie gasped.

'Daddy thinks it was a man at work who wanted his job,' replied Mother, her cheeks flushing pink. 'But Daddy is innocent, and one day everyone will know the truth and he will come home to us.'

Chapter Fourteen

A few weeks later, Bobbie, Phyllis and Peter were on their way back from the station. Perks had finally had a chance to fix Peter's engine, and it was as good as new. Peter could not wait to show it to Jim, who had become a real friend over the few weeks he had been staying with them. Peter was going to join the same school as Jim next year, and it was fun to hear about all the activities he would get to do

– although he was not sure if he wanted to take part in the paper chase.

Bobbie, Peter and Phyllis were chattering away when they noticed a rather grand car parked outsidc their house, with a smart chauffeur standing beside it. 'Who does that belong to?' Peter asked.

They looked at each other before hurrying inside. Mother was in the kitchen preparing a tray of tea things. 'There you are!' she said, cheerfully. 'You are just in time to meet Jim's grandfather. He heard what happened and wanted to come and see how he was getting along.' Mother had a strange smile on her face. It was the same smile she wore whenever she had a surprise for them all.

'What is it?' Bobbie asked. 'Why are you smiling?'

'You'll see,' she said, handing

the tray to Bobbie. 'Why don't you take that up to Jim?'

Bobbie carefully carried the tray upstairs, with Peter and Phyllis close behind her. As they opened the bedroom door, they saw the Old Gentleman sitting by Jim's bed. 'It's you!' Bobbie cried, happily.

'You are Jim's grandfather!'

The Old Gentleman chuckled. 'I am!' he replied. 'Although I prefer to call him James.'

Jim rolled his eyes, good-naturedly.

'I hear you have been taking good care of my grandson,' the Old Gentleman said to Bobbie.

'We all have!' said Phyllis, delighted that the Old Gentleman was in their house. 'Are you staying for tea?'

The Old Gentleman laughed again. 'I would be delighted, young miss.'

In fact, the Old Gentleman stayed all day and only left when the sun was setting. Bobbie walked him to his car and, when she was certain she would not be overheard, summoned up all her courage to tell the Old Gentleman about Father.

The Old Gentleman smiled at her. 'Ever since I found out who you were all those months ago, I have been making enquiries about your father,' he said.

Bobbie's heart began to beat so

SUMMON

To bring into existence or readiness.

loudly that she was certain the Old Gentleman could hear it.

'I never believed he was guilty, you see,' he continued. 'I have employed my best people to look into the case and ...' He paused and looked into Bobbie's eyes.

'I believe there is reason to hope.'

Bobbie threw her arms around the Old Gentleman. 'Oh, thank you!' she cried. 'Thank you! Thank you!'

Chapter Fifteen

When Jim's leg was better, he was sent back to school – which none of the children were happy about. As they said their goodbyes, Jim promised to write to Bobbie.

One morning while they were clearing away the breakfast things, Phyllis said, 'We never talk about Daddy anymore, do we?'

Bobbie's heart sank. Ever since she had discovered where Father was, she had been trying not to mention him in case the secret slipped out. Her little sister studied her feet and Peter stared out of the window. 'I miss him,' he said.

'I know!' said Bobbie, as cheerfully as she could. 'Why don't we send our love to Father on the 9.15 like we used to? We haven't waved to the train in such a long time.'

Peter and Phyllis agreed, and they made it to their spot on the hill just in time to see the train chugging past. They waved their handkerchiefs as usual, but when they looked at the train they noticed something very strange indeed. Every single passenger was waving back and cheering at the three children. In the final carriage was the Old Gentleman, smiling and waving harder than ever.

'How odd!' said Phyllis, delighted at what had just happened.

'Very!' said Peter.

'They must have missed us,' said Bobbie.

Bobbie could not get the train out of her head, and she could not concentrate during her lessons later that day. 'Are you all right, Bobbie dear?' asked Mother.

'Not really,' replied Bobbie. 'I feel sort of … funny. Would you mind if I went for a walk?'

Mother did not mind at all, and Bobbie decided to stroll down to the village. There, she was met by Doctor Forrest. 'Congratulations, my dear!' he said, patting her warmly on the shoulder. 'I must dash, but I am so happy for you all!'

Bobbie had no idea what Doctor Forrest was talking about, but she thanked him all the same. Her feet found their way to the train station, where Perks rushed to greet her. 'You're just in time!' he said. 'Next train, I reckon!'

'Just in time for what?' asked Bobbie, but Perks had already run off to meet the train that was pulling into the station. As the steam cleared, Bobbie watched a lady with a shopping basket step off the train. Then she gasped as a figure who was more recognisable to her than any other person on earth stepped off behind her.

'Daddy!' she cried, running up the platform. 'Daddy, my Daddy!'

Bobbie flew into her father's arms and squeezed him as tightly as she could. It was like a dream. 'Daddy, is it really you?'

'Yes, my darling girl,' Father said, hugging her tightly.

Father and Bobbie walked arm-in-arm to the Three Chimneys.

'Did you not get my letter?' Father asked. 'I wrote to tell you all.'

Bobbie shook her head. 'There was no post this morning,' she said. 'Otherwise I am sure we would have all been at the station to greet you.'

'In that case, you must go into the house first and calmly tell Mother that I have come home,' Father said. 'It might be quite a shock. Tell her they have caught the man who really did it, and everyone knows I am innocent.'

'*I* always knew you were,' Bobbie said, squeezing her father's arm.

When they reached the Three Chimneys, Father waited at the gate while Bobbie rushed into the house. After a moment, Peter and Phyllis ran out and jumped into their father's arms, followed by Mother, who seemed overcome with happiness. Then, wrapped around each other, the family went inside and closed the door.

And that is where we will leave them. The family together at last. A mother and father, and the Railway Children.

Edith Nesbit

Edith Nesbit was born in London in 1858. In an attempt to cure Nesbit's sister's illness, the family lived and travelled a lot of Europe when Nesbit was young. Her family finally settled in Kent, England. Nesbit had a clear talent for poetry that was spotted in her teens. Her further success as a writer meant Nesbit dedicated most of her life to writing for children and adults. *The Railway Children* was published in 1906 at the height of her career.